Just Socks

Mary-Lee Blemings

Illustrated by: Kyle Fleming

Website: mlblemings.wixsite.com/mysite

Weblog: mondayswithmaryhome.wordpress.com

Contact: mlblemings@gmail.com

Illustrations: Kyle Fleming

Printed in Canada

Print ISBN: : 978-1-9990711-1-0

'Just Socks' tells the real-life story of George Kirkham, a homesteader in the Parry Sound District of Ontario. He was also a lumberjack and a WW1 soldier with the 162 Battalion

Dedicated to all those who knew George Kirkham as 'Popop'

ROBO MAN!
ROBOT MAN
NEW
SUPER CAR

R ILEY COULD NOT believe his eyes. He had been looking forward to opening the present from his grandpa, or Papa Dave as he called him, but this was more than disappointing. "Just socks!" he exclaimed, throwing the package across the room.

Riley's mother, Lindsay, was not happy with her son's behaviour. "Riley Cole," she snapped, "That's rude! Now apologize to your grandfather!"

"But…," he stammered.

"Oh, that's okay," Papa Dave said. "He didn't mean any harm, did you?"

"No, it is *not* okay," Lindsay insisted. "Now, off you go to your room, young man. You need to think about what is right. No more presents until you can say sorry, and mean it."

Riley stomped off. "That's not fair!" he shouted back at them as he climbed the stairs.

Papa Dave rose slowly from his chair. "Let me see what I can do, Lindsay," he said to his daughter-in-law.

"No, Dad. Riley needs to learn. He was very rude and he should not get away with that behaviour."

"You are right, but I have an idea. I have my ways, you know."

"Yes, I am sure you can work your magic. Just don't go too easy on him, okay."

The old man climbed the stairs, and shuffled his way down to his grandson's bedroom door. He knocked, and before he got an answer, he stuck his head in the door.

Riley didn't look up. He was lying on top of his bed playing Fortnite on his iPad.

"Can I come in?" Papa Dave asked.

Riley grunted, "I guess," and continued with his game.

His grandpa slid the computer chair over beside the bed. "Want to hear a story?"

Riley finally looked up at his grandpa. "No thanks, Papa. I'm getting a little old for that, don't you think?"

"Actually, I don't think a person is ever too old for a story. I have a good one for you too. It would help pass some time until you are allowed to go back downstairs. Okay?"

Riley just groaned. "I'm sorry. Okay?" He picked

up his iPad again. The tone of his voice did not sound like he was the least bit sorry.

Papa Dave did not take the bait. "Let's get to that later. Meanwhile, I thought you'd like to hear about my grandpa. We called him Popop. His real name was George…George Kirkham. " Papa Dave took a photo from his wallet.

"Here's a photo of him." Papa Dave studied the photo like he had never seen it before.

Riley knew from experience there was no getting out of this. He glanced at the picture, then flopped back on his pillow."Yeah, I know. You show me that picture every Remembrance Day."

"Right, but I've never told you much about my popop, have I? He was a soldier. He was at Vimy

Ridge in WW1." When Riley did not respond, Papa put the photo back in his wallet. "I will tell you more about that later, but first I want to tell you a little about his life on the homestead."

Riley rolled his eyes. "Here we go again," he thought, but did not say aloud. Once Papa started telling a story, there was no stopping him.

It was 1902 when my popop was your age, Riley. He had nine brothers and sisters and they all lived in a farmhouse, in the woods of northern Ontario.

Their home was on the edge of a small lake called Loch Erne.

It didn't take long for Riley to turn over and get interested. He would never admit it, but he did really love his grandpa's tales, even if he was ten years old.

Popop was raised on a farm that his father had built with own hands. Your great great grandfather had bought land by the lake and homesteaded it. Land needed to be cleared of trees and plowed to plant grain and hay crops. As a homesteader Popop's father built roads and fences. He purchased pigs, horses, cows and chickens to raise, but his family also depended a lot on hunting and fishing for food.

"I wish I could go hunting. I think fishing is

boring, but I'd like to go hunting. Uncle Mark says he will take me when I'm older. You should come with us."

"I don't care to hunt," Papa Dave admitted, "but if Uncle wants to teach you, that's okay." Papa shifted to get comfortable and continued the story.

A home was a first priority, so Popop's father chopped down trees, and sawed them into lumber to build the houses, barns and other buildings. He even had to make the furniture- chairs, tables, cupboards and beds for the house. Homesteaders had to be skilled in many areas. Fathers taught their sons how to do things. There was so much work to do, and they were the only ones to do it.

All of the children had chores. The boys often looked after the sheep and pigs, and the girls helped with household duties. The young children might collect eggs, and older girls would milk cows.

"You have some chores, don't you, Riley?"

"Sure. I have to take out the garbage, and walk the dog, and put my dirty clothes in the hamper. My little brother doesn't have to do anything!"

One of George's jobs when he was your age was to tend the sheep. Every day he would take them to the pasture and watch them to protect them from wolves. The sheep were important to the family because they provided wool. Every fall, the neighbours would help each other shear the sheep, and then the women would spin the wool into yarn.

George's mother and sisters used the yarn to knit many articles of clothing-scarves, mitts, sweaters, jackets, and most importantly, socks.

Riley flopped back onto his bed. "Papa, I think I know where this is going? I said sorry! Geez!"

"I'm just telling a story, son. Be patient."

Patience wasn't one of Riley's best qualities. He rolled his eyes again, which he was quite famous for, and rolled over with his back to his grandfather. If he heard the word 'socks' one more time he was going to snap!

Papa Dave was not deterred.

Winters were long and very cold, so warm clothing was absolutely necessary. Warm, dry socks were greatly appreciated. I remember Popop telling us about Christmas at the homestead. They would all go to church on Christmas Eve in the sleigh.

When they got home, the children were allowed to open one of their two presents.

Riley turned back over. "You're telling me they only got two presents? Were they poor or something?"

"I guess you could say that. They grew their own vegetables, they raised their own animals for meat, they made their own clothes, and everything they could, so they did not have to buy things. They had to buy some things obviously, but they certainly didn't have money for extras. Besides, they had to go many kilometres on dirt roads to a town, and did not make a trip like that very often."

Riley just shook his head. He got more than two presents just in his stocking! Living in the olden days didn't sound like much fun!

Popop would always pick the present wrapped in a linen cloth, tied with string, hidden in the branches of the Christmas tree. He knew it would be a special new pair of socks that his mother had knit for him, but he would still pretend to be surprised. He did not have to pretend to be happy. He would wear his new socks to bed. Even though he shared his bed with two younger brothers, his feet would get too cold without soft, warm woollen socks. There was a little stove in the girls' bedroom, but not in the boys'.

"You're kidding, right? Socks again?" Riley was getting annoyed. "You should call this story, 'Just Socks!'" He knew he should apologize properly, and get it over with, but Riley was also known for being stubborn.

Riley's grandfather just grinned at him and went back to the tale.

But even Popop didn't come to really appreciate socks until the year he turned twelve. That was when he no longer had to go to school, and was expected to take on full responsibilities on the farm. Part of this meant that he would go to work in the lumber camps in the forest for much of the winter with his father, older brother and other men in that region.

The women and younger children would remain on the homestead to look after the home and animals. Families needed the extra money the men would earn in the lumber camps because they did not earn enough from their crops to survive.

Life in the camp was hard, damp, and cold work! They toiled long hours doing backbreaking work like building roads, cutting down trees, and loading and hauling trees on wagons. The younger boys got jobs like helping the cook, clearing the trails, shovelling the

horse manure. The work continued dawn to dusk in the rain, wind, snow and freezing temperatures.

At night they would get warm around a wood stove, and try to dry their socks. The socks would steam, but would seldom dry completely overnight.

The many pairs of socks Popop's mother had sent with him were treasured. Some of his cabin mates were not as lucky to have a mother or wife to knit for them. Popop would bring extra pairs to share.

Riley sat up and frowned. "Your popop got to quit school when he was twelve? Cool! But how come he had to work so much? He was just a kid."

Papa Dave leaned back in his chair and crossed his arms across his chest. "Yes, he was. But it was a very different time. Every member of the family needed to help. His father always said he was lucky to have so many children."

This was Popop's life for ten years. Work on the farm, and work in the lumber camp. He grew strong, and earned a reputation for being a quick learner and a hard worker.

There were fun times, of course. Neighbours visited and helped each other. For example, if someone needed a barn built, men from the farms around would come to help. It was called a barn-raising. The children would play, and women would cook a big feast. It would be a day everyone loved.

Sunday was also a day the family enjoyed. The church was built on land close by that George's dad had donated. Church was a time for neighbours to get together. People often visited each other to share meals after the service . Sometimes there would be a social. Local men would bring their fiddles, harmonicas and juice harps, and adults and children alike would join in the singing and dancing.

"That does sound like fun! What's a juice harp?"

"It's a little piece of metal you put in your mouth, and you can make music with it. We could look it up on the internet if you like?"

"Okay. Later."

Popop might have lived his whole life this way-clearing and farming the land, raising animals and working in the woods every winter. But something was happening in the world that would change every-thing. My popop, George Kirkham, would not live a homesteader's life any longer.

Papa Dave reached for Riley's iPad. He did a quick search, then showed his grandson a poster.

"This is what I'm talking about."

Across the ocean, in Europe, a war had broken out. We call it World War 1 or the Great War. Britain and her allies (partners) were fighting against Germany to keep people free. Canada was one of Britain's allies, so many Canadian young men were joining the army to help.

They thought the war would not last long, but they were in for a big surprise. Two years after it started, so many men had been lost or injured that more and more recruits were needed.

"I'd go!" Riley said. He was sitting up on the edge of his bed now, pretending to shoot a rifle. "Did George and all his brothers sign up?"

"It wasn't that simple, Riley. Remember what I said about everyone being needed on the farm? What would Popop s father do if all his sons went off to war? He couldn't possibly do all the work on the homestead himself."

"Your popop went though, didn't he?"

"Yes, he had gone to the recruitment meetings and had heard about the great need for soldiers. Many of his friends had already signed up. He knew he would meet all the requirements to be accepted."

THIS IS YOUR FLAG
IT STANDS FOR LIBERTY
FIGHT FOR IT
JOIN THE
OVERSEAS BATTALION
OTTAWA-CARLETON BATTALION
207
JOIN THE OVERSEAS BATTALION
LT. COL. C.W. MAC LEAN,
Officer Commanding.
APPLY BASE RECRUITING OFFICE
SPARKS ST. OTTAWA.

Farmers were needed to supply the troops with grain and other food, so the army said only one son from each farm family would have to go to war. Popop signed up so his brothers could stay on the farm. It would be an adventure!

Soon he was off to training in the local town, and then at a camp near Niagara Falls. Having grown up on the farm and working in the lumber camp had prepared him for many of the required skills. He was in good physical shape, so the fitness training was not too bad. He also knew how to use a rifle, but he had to practice his marksmanship. He learned new skills: how to live out of a backpack, how to use a bayonet, and how to throw a grenade.

Of course, learning to follow orders is very important in the military. Popop was not too happy with that in the beginning.

"People generally don't like taking orders, do they, Riley?" His grandson smirked but did not answer.

Another part of the training that took some getting used to was the need for constant drills and long marches. Daily marches, sometimes up to thirty kilometres, were required, and that was very hard on the feet. The officers would regularly check that the men had plenty of...

"I know….socks! Papa, you don't have to keep bringing that up." Riley whined.

"Oh, but I do. Socks were essential, so they didn't get blisters and sores. They had to walk everywhere, and they certainly couldn't march with sore feet."

After six months of training, Popop was granted leave to go home to the farm and help with harvest before he was sent overseas. His family was very proud to see him in his new uniform. There was a community social to send him off, and that is where he met Blanche, his future wife. They liked each other right away, and she promised to write to him while he was gone.

"That's kind of romantic, isn't it?" Papa Dave grinned. "Would you like to see some of the post-cards he sent? They are like emails on paper,"

"I know what a postcard is, Papa," Riley answered, sarcastically, "And no I don't want to read any mushy stuff. Can we get back to the war part now?"

Soon, Popop traveled by train with his fellow soldiers to Halifax. Then he boarded a ship, called the Caronia, which would take him to England.

The voyage was not nearly as pleasant as he had expected. It was very crowded, and the Atlantic was

often rough. Eleven days later, Popop was very happy to see the shores of Ireland. From there he traveled by train to Folkstone, England, where he would have three more weeks of training. He had lots more to learn.

Finally, Popop was sent to the front lines in France. He had been transferred to the 2nd Pioneer Battalion. No one could have been prepared for the realities of trench warfare that he became a part of.

WW1 was like a long siege. The opposing armies had dug in trenches and tunnels, and from these positions, they faced one another in a standoff. The space between them was called 'No Man's Land.' There were massive artillery bombardments and some infantry advances and raids, but neither side was making much headway. There had been huge battles before Popop arrived at the front. Over 700,000 men had already died, and over a million had been injured.

Popop arrived just as the Canadian Corp was preparing for the battle at Vimy Ridge. As part of the Pioneers he was right in the middle of the action. The Pioneers supported the front line troops. His duties were to construct and repair trenches, to build and repair roads, and to lay barbed wire. He even had to

help move bodies to a cemetery for burial-not his favourite job.

Popop told me he made good friends with the men in his section. They ate, slept, sang, chatted, played cards, and shared letters together. It was a little like life back at the lumber camp. At night they would return to their shelter at the rear of the trenches. Of course, the clay floor would have turned to mud because of the constant heavy rainfall.

Mud was everywhere! It covered their bodies, their clothing, and their bedding. Popop would crawl into bed with his dirty, wet clothes on because the soldiers were not allowed to take them off. The mud would just dry and stick there.

As you can imagine, staying safe and healthy was difficult. Comfort was impossible. Sometimes the walls of the trench would collapse. Many times soldiers became trapped in the thick, deep mud and never got out.

"Yuk! That's horrible!" Riley said. "I actually can't imagine that."

"You're right. We have no idea what the soldiers went through. But wait until you hear this."

Creatures like rats, frogs, beetles and slugs shared

their space and were more than a nuisance; they were a source of disease. Popop's body was usually covered in lice, and he was lucky he did not get trench fever which was caused by the lice. Trench fever is very painful and it takes months to recover from it.

Riley started scratching his head. "Just the thought of lice makes me itch!"

Another common injury was trench foot, which is sort of like frostbite. A man might develop trench foot because he was forced to stand in water in the trenches for several hours or even days without being able to remove wet socks and boots. Socks had to be changed daily. A friend of George's, Billy, had an extreme case of trench foot and had to have several toes amputated.

This time Riley did not protest the socks comment.

Popop made sure to look after his feet. He rubbed them with whale oil and tried to put fresh socks on at least once a day.

There was a plentiful supply of socks, sent by the Red Cross, but the ones his mother sent from home that first Christmas were like gold. No other gift could compare. Popop told me he would close his eyes and picture his mom sitting in her rocking chair, knitting.

Papa Dave did not make eye contact with Riley, who was unusually quiet.

At night, curled up in a hole in the damp ground, with the rats running over him in search of biscuits, Popop would listen to the wail of shells overhead and the sound of machine guns. He was no longer excited about this adventure.

In later years, Popop remembered the artillery bombardment as the most terrifying experience of the war. He would hear the whine or shriek grow louder until at last, it burst with an ear-splitting explosion. It would dig a hole a meter deep in the ground and about three meters in diameter. It threw dirt, stones, and anything else it came in contact with forty meters into the air. He and his crew would crowd into a dugout and wait for the crash. They would feel a tremendous pressure, and when it was over, they would crawl out of the hole and get back to work.

One time, Popop was not so lucky. The shell crashed right in the dugout where he was taking cover. He was covered in mud, but alive. They dug him out, bandaged his wound, and carried him on a stretcher to a first-aid post. He had a broken leg and was sent to a Canadian hospital in England to recover. He had what they called a 'blighty'-an injury severe enough to get him away from the front, but one that would heal in time.

After his fracture healed, he remained in the hospital as a 'walking patient' while he waited to be sent back to France. Back to war.

The Red Cross people provided him with toiletries and came to visit him.He and other patients were taught to knit to help pass the time. At one time Popop might have thought knitting was women's work, but he had changed his mind. He was proud to be doing something so important. He was knitting socks for soldiers.

As it turned out, Popop was never sent back to the front. In the early summer of 1918, he came down with a deadly illness, the Spanish Flu, that many people worldwide were dying from. But again, Popop was lucky. He survived and just before he was to be sent back to the Western Front, he was even more fortunate. The miracle that so many had been praying for was to take place. Peace and Armistice were signed on November 11,1918. The Great War was over.

"The eleventh hour of the eleventh day of the eleventh month. That's what my teacher said."

Papa Dave gave him the thumbs-up sign and smiled. "Remembrance Day."

George came home to Canada, where he later married and had eight children. He didn't go back to farming. He decided to live in the town of Port Credit on Lake Ontario.

"That's where you lived too, right?"

He and Grandma lived right next door when I was a boy. We kids played in his home and his yard as if they were our own. He grew the biggest garden on the block. He also supervised the building of our family cabins up at Loch Erne. Popop knew a lot about construction because his father had taught him when he was very young.

My popop spent a lot of time outside in his Muskoka chair, and I often played crib with him there in the shade by the snowball tree. We talked a bit, but he didn't talk about the war too much. His son, Bruce, had died in a plane crash, and my grandma died soon after that. Popop didn't talk about that either. Maybe he didn't want to frighten me or make me sad.

"If he didn't tell you too much, how do you know all this stuff?" Riley was seriously interested. It was a good question.

"I did quite a bit of research. I'm very interested in history, especially family history. Now, let me tell you the end of this story. Can you guess what it's about?"

"I'm thinking it's got something to do with socks." Riley had a big smile on his face.

"You're a clever kid! Yes, and it's about Christmas too. We can't forget what day this is!"

Every Christmas, a package from Popop was under the tree. We always knew that present was socks. Every year Popop gave each of us kids a pair of socks, that he had knit himself. He had never been one to sit and watch TV. On days he couldn't go outside he preferred to sit on his cot and sometimes listen to the radio. Often he would get his knitting needles and a ball of wool and just sit there and knit for hours.

On Christmas morning, I remember opening Popop's gift last. I knew what was inside. It was no big deal, I thought. It was 'just socks', so I left it by the tree and went to play with a new, more exciting present.

"You did? You said 'just socks' like I did?"

"No, I wouldn't have dared say that aloud.

I'd have got my ears boxed! But I did think it… and he probably knew what I was thinking, if you know what I mean."

Riley remained quiet.

Papa looked him straight in the eye. "You know what I wish I had right now, more than anything in the world?"

Riley said nothing. He could see the sadness in his grandfather's eyes. Maybe now was a good time to say sorry.

"I wish I still had a pair of my grandpa's homemade socks."

Riley didn't know what to say.

Just then, Lindsay, Riley's mom, stuck her head in the bedroom door. "Everything settled? Have you apologized, young man?" she asked.

"Yes. It's all good," Papa Dave said. He got up, stretched and ambled towards the door.

"Your cousins are arriving, Riley. You better come downstairs now," Lindsay called, as she hurried back downstairs.

Riley called after her, "I'll be down in a minute, okay?" Then he turned to his grandpa."Thanks… Popop," he whispered.

The doorbell rang, and the entrance filled with the bustle of cousins, uncles, and aunts.

Everyone was hugging and laughing and saying, 'Merry Christmas'.

Only Papa Dave noticed what Riley, his grand-son, was wearing when he came down the stairs.

About the Author

Mary-Lee Blemings, a retired teacher, is a mother, grandma, and great-grandma. She has a great love for children, animals, nature, music, art, Canadian history and family ancestry. Dave Blemings, her husband, is Papa Dave in this story.

About the Illustrator

Kyle Fleming lives a quiet life in the middle of the forest in a tiny off-grid house he and his wife built by hand. A lifelong freelance illustrator and artist, Kyle can be contacted through his website:

https://kyleflemingsart.weebly.com

Also by Mary-Lee Blemings

Also by this author is her first children's novel, 'The (Not So) True Story of the Ralston School Herman'. This humorous and touching story is based on the legendary creature who inhabits the tunnels beneath a military school, the author once taught at. Emma Dawn, renowned liar and troublemaker, discovers Herman's true identity. Will she keep his secret?

Available at Amazon.ca